ABIGAIL
at the beach

Felix Pirani · pictures by Christine Roche

Dial Books for Young Readers · New York

Abigail and her daddy went to the beach.

Abigail's daddy took an umbrella and a
beach chair and a Thermos full of orange juice
and three cans of ice-cold soda and a box of
cookies and a book.

Abigail took a pail and a shovel.
Abigail's daddy put up the umbrella and
put the beach chair under it. He sat down and
started to read his book.

Abigail began to build the biggest castle in the
world. First she built four towers for the corners.

The towers were so far apart that you could
barely see from one to the next, and each one
was so high that it would take you a day and
a half to climb to the top.

Two boys came walking along the beach. "Hey, look at those!" said one of them to the other. "Bet I can knock down one of those piles of sand quicker than you can."

"You touch one of my towers," said Abigail,
"and I'll get my daddy to hang you both
upside down by the heels. He's in the Mob."

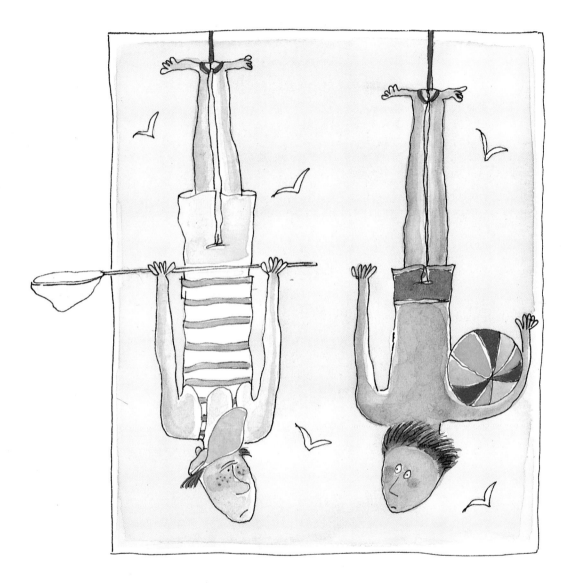

The two boys walked on down the beach.
"Look, Daddy," said Abigail. "Look at
what I've built!"
"What on earth are those?" asked
her daddy.
"Can't you *see*?" said Abigail. "They're
the corner towers of the biggest
castle in the world."
"It's going to be enormous," said
her daddy.
"Would you like this empty soda can?"

"Yes, please," said Abigail. She put the soda can
on top of one of the towers. It made a wonderful
lookout. From up there you'd be able to
see all the ships in the sea for fifty miles around.

Abigail's daddy opened another can of soda
and turned the page.
"What's happening in your book?" asked
Abigail.
"The Martians have landed, but they haven't
gotten out of their spaceship yet," said her daddy.

Abigail built the walls for the biggest castle in the world. The walls were so broad that you could have landed two spaceships side by side on top without them touching.

"I bet I can ride through that pile of sand
without getting stuck," he said to Abigail.

Abigail built the walls for the biggest castle in the world. The walls were so broad that you could have landed two spaceships side by side on top without them touching.

A boy came riding along the beach on a bicycle.

"I bet I can ride through that pile of sand without getting stuck," he said to Abigail.

"You go anywhere near my castle," said Abigail, "and I'll get my daddy to break both your arms and frazzle your bike. He's in the Secret Service."

The boy rode off.
"Look, Daddy," said Abigail. "Look at what
I've built!"
"What's all that?" asked her daddy.

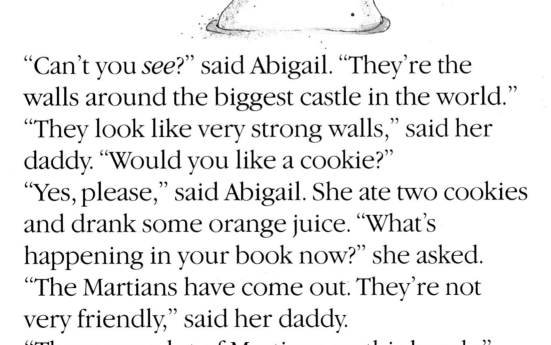

"Can't you *see*?" said Abigail. "They're the walls around the biggest castle in the world." "They look like very strong walls," said her daddy. "Would you like a cookie?" "Yes, please," said Abigail. She ate two cookies and drank some orange juice. "What's happening in your book now?" she asked. "The Martians have come out. They're not very friendly," said her daddy. "There are a lot of Martians on this beach," said Abigail.

Abigail dug a moat around the biggest castle
in the world to keep the Martians out. It was
deep enough and wide enough to fit a
ferryboat, and it had a great drawbridge
so that you could let other people across.

Two girls came running along the beach.
They had a dog on a leash.

The dog stopped and started to dig
under the drawbridge.
"You keep your dog away from my castle,"
said Abigail, "or I'll get my daddy to shoot
a lot of holes in it. He's in the Marines."

The two girls dragged the dog
away and went off.

"Look, Daddy," said Abigail. "Look at what I've done."
"What is it?" asked her daddy.
"Can't you *see*?" said Abigail.

"It's a moat around the biggest castle in the world."
"It ought to keep Martians out," said her daddy.

"It seems that they're afraid of water.

"Would you like another soda can?"
"Yes, please," said Abigail. The soda can
made a useful submarine in the moat in
case any Martians tried to cross on rafts.

Abigail built a great bell tower in the middle
of the biggest castle in the world. It was even
higher than the other towers, so that the spire
was often hidden in the clouds.

It was going to have the biggest bell in the world.
When it was rung, you would be able to hear it
halfway to China.

"That's a high tower," said Abigail's daddy. "What's it for?"

"Can't you *see*?" said Abigail. "It's the bell tower."

"Here's the bell," said her daddy, and gave her the last soda can.

"How far is it around your castle?"

"Ten miles," said Abigail.

"What shall I call it?"

"Xanadu," said her daddy. "Xanadu with an X.
Have you finished yet?" he asked.
"We could go home for supper."
"Yes," said Abigail. "I've had
a wonderful time – can
we come back tomorrow?"
"Yes," said her daddy,
"but you know, the tide
might wash it away
by tomorrow."

"I know," said Abigail, "but I'm going to build
a better one tomorrow."